Ms. Hall Is a Goofball!

Dan Gutman

Pictures by
Jim Paillot

HARPER
An Imprint of HarperCollinsPublishers

Special thanks to
Tommy Gemma and Terry Sirrell

My Weirdest School #12: Ms. Hall Is a Goofball!
Text copyright © 2018 by Dan Gutman
Illustrations copyright © 2018 by Jim Paillot

ISBN 978-0-06-242945-2 (pbk. bdg.)—ISBN 978-0-06-242946-9 (library bdg.)

Typography by Laura Mock
19 20 21 22   CG/BRR   10 9 8 7 6
❖
First Edition

Contents

Big News!

My name is A.J. and I hate current events.

Do you know what current events are? In Mr. Cooper's class, once a week we have to bring in an article we cut out of the newspaper. Then we have to stand in front of the class and talk about it.

So the other day, we had current events, and I forgot to bring in an article.

1

Everybody got up and talked about their current event.

Andrea Young, this annoying girl with curly brown hair, talked about some furry animals that might go extinct.

Michael, who never ties his shoes, talked about last week's pro football games.

Ryan, who will eat anything, talked about some new food that nobody ever heard of.

Alexia, this girl who rides a skateboard all the time, talked about a new skate park that's opening up.

Neil, who we call the nude kid even though he wears clothes, talked about the Statue of Liberty. It has a poem on it that says, "Give me your tired, your poor, your huddled masses yearning to breathe free."*

I was hoping Mr. Cooper wouldn't call on me. So instead of looking at him, I looked at the floor. If you don't want the teacher to call on you, always look at the floor. That's the first rule of being a kid.

"Your turn, A.J.," said Mr. Cooper.

Bummer in the summer! I didn't know what to say. I didn't know what to do. I had to think fast.

"My dog ate my current event," I said.

"A.J.," Mr. Cooper replied, "you don't have a dog."

---

*Wow, I didn't know so many people had respiratory problems.

Oh, yeah.

"That's the third time in a row that you forgot to bring in a current event, A.J."

"Well," I told Mr. Cooper, "it doesn't make sense that we have to do current events anyway. Current events are happening right *now*, and you can't bring them in because they're too busy happening. If you ask me, they shouldn't be called current events because once they're in the newspaper, they're not current anymore. They should be called *old* events."

Mr. Cooper started rubbing his forehead with his fingers. Grown-ups do that all the time. Nobody knows why. Maybe they need a head massage.

Speaking of heads, you'll never believe who poked his head into the door at that moment.

Nobody! Doors are made of wood. Why would you poke your head into a piece of wood?

But you'll never believe who poked his head into the door*way*.

It was Mr. Klutz, our principal! He has no hair at all. I mean *none*. He would be taller if he had some hair on top of his head.

"Did I hear somebody say current events aren't current?" he said. "Well, I have some news, and it just happened a minute ago."

"What is it?" we all asked.

"Ms. LaGrange is leaving us."

"*Nooooooooooo!*" we all shouted.

Ms. LaGrange is our lunch lady. She's from France, and she always says weird words like *bonjour*, whatever *that* means. She also writes secret messages in the mashed potatoes. Ms. LaGrange is strange.

When they heard that she was leaving, everybody started yelling and screaming and shrieking and hooting and hollering and freaking out.

Mr. Klutz held up his hand and made a peace sign with his fingers, which means "shut up!"

"Ms. LaGrange is going back to France,"

he told us. "She's being deported."

Nobody knew what that meant, so Little Miss I-Know-Everything looked it up on her smartphone. Deported is when they take some of those tired, poor people who can't breathe and send them back where they came from.

"Gotta run," said Mr. Klutz. "I have to go find a new lunch lady!"

Lunch Is My Life

After all the excitement was over, Mr. Cooper told us to turn to page twenty-three in our math books. But nobody could pay attention to math. We were all sad about Ms. LaGrange. She was nice.

"How is Mr. Klutz going to find a new lunch lady?" asked Emily, who is Andrea's crybaby friend.

"He'll probably go to Rent-A-Lunch Lady," I replied. "You can rent anything."

Mr. Cooper told us to stop chatting and turn back to page twenty-three in our math books. But you'll never believe who poked his head into the door at that moment.

Nobody! It would hurt if you poked your head into a door. I thought we went over that in Chapter One.

But you'll never believe who poked his head into the door*way*.

It was Mr. Klutz *again*!

"Guess what?" he asked.

"Your butt?" I replied. Any time any-body asks what's up, you should always reply "your butt." That's the first rule of being a kid.

"I found our new lunch lady!" Mr. Klutz said excitedly.

Wow, *that* was fast!

At that moment, the weirdest thing in the history of the world happened. Some lady came roller-skating into the room. She was wearing a white uniform with an apron over it and yellow rubber gloves. Her hair looked like it was gray, but it was almost blue. And she was wearing a net over her hair, like she needed to catch some fish or something.

"Hi everybody!" the lady said. "I'm Ms. Hall!"

Mr. Klutz told us that when he went
outside to look for a new lunch lady, Ms.
Hall happened to be roller-skating down
the street. So he hired her on the spot.

Huh! How often does *that* happen?

"I'm so excited to be your new lunch lady," Ms. Hall told us. "Lunch is my life. You know how everybody says breakfast is the most important meal of the day? Well, I think that's wrong. Breakfast is way overrated. I say *lunch* is the most important meal of the day."

Wow, she's really passionate about ranking the meals of the day.

"Welcome to Ella Mentry School, Ms. Hall," said Mr. Klutz. "What will you be making us for lunch today?"

"Veggies," she replied. "Lots of veggies!"

Oh no! Not veggies! People who eat veggies are plant eaters. I'm not going to eat plants.

"I love veggies!" shouted Andrea, who loves everything I hate.

"Me too!" shouted Emily, who loves everything Andrea loves.

"That's great!" said Ms. Hall. "Veggies are very important for good health. Did you know that obesity rates have more than tripled since the 1970s? I think the solution to the problem is to get kids eating more veggies."

"Obesity?" I asked. "What's obesity?"

"That's when beasts come to the city," said Michael.

"Stop trying to scare Emily," said Andrea.

"There are beasts in the city?" asked Emily. "I'm scared."

"Help!" hollered Neil. "The beasts are coming! Call 911!"

"Run for your lives!" yelled Ryan.

Everybody started yelling and screaming and shrieking and hooting and hollering and freaking out.

"We've got to *do* something!" shouted Emily. Then she went running out of the room.

Sheesh, get a grip! That girl will fall for anything.

Mystery Meat and Nofu

After that, we had to go to science class.

"Pringle up, everybody!" said Mr. Cooper.

We lined up in single file and walked a million hundred miles to the science room.

Our science teacher is Mr. Docker. But when we got to the science room, Mr. Docker was talking with the computer teacher, Mrs. Yonkers; the new lunch lady, Ms. Hall; and Mr. Harrison, the guy who fixes the copy machines and stuff when it breaks.

"Good morning," said Mr. Docker. "In honor of our new lunch lady, Ms. Hall, today we're going to talk about some exciting new developments in food technology. Mr. Harrison, would you like to start things off?"

Mr. Harrison went up to the front of the room. He had a little white thing in his hand, but I couldn't tell what it was.

"I've been working in my workshop on this new tool that you kids will be able to use in the lunchroom," he explained.

"What is that thing?" asked Mr. Docker.

"You know what a spork is, right?" said Mr. Harrison. "It's a spoon and a fork all in one. Well, I've developed a *new* utensil. It's a fork, knife, *and* spoon all in one."

"That's very interesting," said Mr. Docker. "What do you call it?"

"I call it a knoof," said Mr. Harrison. "Knife, spoon, and fork."

"How do you spell 'knoof'?" asked Andrea, who always cares about how words are spelled just in case they'll be on a spelling test someday. What is her problem?

"*K-N-O-O-F*," he replied. "The *K* is silent."*

---

*If the *K* is silent, why is it there? If you ask me, they should get rid of the letter *K*.

"That's a great idea!" said Ms. Hall. "I can't wait to try out a knoof at lunch today."

We all clapped our hands in circles to give Mr. Harrison a round of applause.

"Okay, Ms. Hall, you have the floor," said Mr. Docker.

That was weird. What does she need the floor for? Who wants a floor anyway?

Ms. Hall held up a plate full of cupcakes. Yum!

"Thank you," she said. "I wanted to give the kids a sneak peek at my new recipe: meatball cupcakes with mashed potato icing!"

"That sounds yummy!" said Andrea.

"I agree," said Emily, who agrees with everything Andrea says.

"Gross!" I said. "What kind of meat is in a meatball cupcake?"

"Mystery meat," said Ms. Hall.

"What's mystery meat?" we all asked.

"If I told you, it wouldn't be a mystery," said Ms. Hall.

That was weird. We all clapped our hands in circles to give Ms. Hall a round of applause.

Next it was Mrs. Yonkers's turn. She picked up a few plates that were on the windowsill.

"As you know, it's important for kids to eat veggies," said Mrs. Yonkers. "So Mr.

Docker and I have been working in the lab. We came up with a few ideas."

Mr. Docker held up a box of Twinkies.

"*Now* you're talking my language!" I said. "I love Twinkies!"

"Oh, these aren't Twinkies," Mr. Docker said. "They're *Vinkies*. We took regular Twinkies, scooped out the cream filling, and put veggies in there instead. You're gonna love 'em!"

"That's a great idea!" said Ms. Hall.

Ugh, gross! Veggie-filled Twinkies? I thought I was gonna throw up.

Next Mrs. Yonkers held up a big green pepper.

"It looks like a regular pepper, right?" she said, cutting it open with a knife. "But

it's not a regular pepper. There's a little toy inside. See? We can grow the pepper right around the toy!"

"Amazing!" said Ms. Hall. "So it's sort of like a Happy Meal."

More like a Sad Meal, if you ask me.

"And *this* is our masterpiece," Mr. Docker said, holding up some white thing. "You've heard of tofu, right?"

"I love tofu!" said Andrea and a few other kids.

Ugh, gross! I'm not eating food made out of toes. Why can't a truck full of tofu fall on Andrea's head?

"For many people, tofu is an alternative to meat," said Mr. Docker. "But some people don't like tofu. That's why we've developed this new food—nofu."

Nofu?

"Yes, nofu is an alternative to tofu," explained Mrs. Yonkers. "It's tofu with no tofu in it, for people who don't like tofu."

"So it's tofu free," said Mr. Docker. "You're gonna love it!"

"I love it *already*!" said Ms. Hall.

"Not only that," continued Mrs. Yonkers. "Our sense of smell is connected to our sense of taste, so we've developed a new product that you spray on veggies to make them taste and smell like meat."

Mr. Docker took a can of something and sprayed it on a piece of nofu.

"See?" he said. "It's canned meat spray!"

"It's like portable meat in a can!" said Mrs. Yonkers.

Ms. Hall picked up the piece of nofu with

meat spray on it and took a bite.

"Mmmm!" she said. "Veggie meat! It's delicious! I *love* it!"

Portable meat spray in a can? Ugh. All that stuff sounded horrible.

And those teachers are weird.

My Name Is A.J. and I Hate Veggies

I wasn't all that excited for lunch the next day as we walked a million hundred miles to the vomitorium.* I was the line leader. Ms. Hall greeted us at the door.

"Hi dollface!" she said to me.

---

*It used to be called the cafetorium. But then some first grader threw up in there.

"Dollface?" I asked. "Why are you calling me dollface?"

"No reason," she said. "Hey, look! I installed an all-you-can-eat salad bar!"

"What if all I want to eat is *no* salad?" I asked. "The only bar I like is a candy bar. You should have an all-you-can-eat *candy* bar."

"Hmm," Ms. Hall replied. "What if I sprayed the salad with some portable meat?"

"No thank you," I told her. "I brought my lunch from home. Can I just have a bunch of straws? I always carry extra straws with me."

"Sure, dollface," she said. "Why do you

carry straws with you?"

"Because whenever I do something," I told her, "grown-ups are always saying that's the last straw."

I had a peanut butter and jelly sandwich. So did Ryan, Michael, Neil, and Alexia. You *have* to eat a peanut butter and jelly sandwich for lunch every day. That's the law.

Andrea and Emily, of course, went to the all-you-can-eat salad bar.

"I love veggies," Andrea said when she came back to the table.

"Me too," said Emily.

"My favorite veggie is cauliflower," Andrea said.

"Mine too," said Emily.

Ugh. I'm not going to eat *any* kind of a flower.

"What's *your* favorite vegetable, Arlo?" asked Andrea, who calls me by my real name because she knows I don't like it.

"Twinkies," I said.

"Twinkies aren't a vegetable!" Andrea told me.

"Well, they *should* be," I replied.

We all started eating our lunches.

"I don't think I'm going to like Ms. Hall," said Alexia. "I hate veggies."

"Me too," said Michael.

"Me three," I said.

My favorite thing to do at lunch is annoy Emily.

"Hey Emily," I said. "Do you like sea-food?"

"Sure!" she said. "I *love* seafood!"

I took a bite of my peanut butter and jelly sandwich. Then I chewed it a little. Then I opened my mouth wide so Emily could look inside.

"See?" I said. "Food!"

"Ewwww, gross!" Emily said.

"Stop trying to scare Emily," Andrea told me.

"Hey, maybe Ms. Hall isn't

a *real* lunch lady," I said. "Did you ever think of that?"

"What do you mean?" asked Alexia.

"Well," I said, "maybe Ms. LaGrange wasn't *really* sent back to France. Maybe Ms. Hall kidnapped her."

"I'm scared," said Emily.

"Yeah," said Ryan. "Maybe Ms. Hall locked Ms. LaGrange up in the freezer. Stuff like that happens all the time, you know."

"We've got to *do* something!" Emily shouted. And then she went running out of the room.

Sheesh! That girl will fall for just about *anything*.

"That wasn't nice, Arlo!" Andrea told me.

"Well, she started it," I replied. "She said she liked seafood."

Actually I like seafood too. One time, Ryan and I were at his house playing video games, and we decided we were hungry for shrimp lo mein. So we decided to dig a hole to China so we could get Chinese food. We got a couple of feet down before we got tired and decided to go inside and play video games again. Ryan's mom said we worked really hard, so she took us out for shrimp lo mein.

Yum! I love Chinese food. And the best part is, you don't have to dig a hole to China to eat it.

While we were eating, Ms. Hall came over to our table. She was holding a big zucchini. It looked like a baseball bat.

"I just wanted to see how you kids were making out," she said.

"Eww, gross!" we all shouted. "We're not making out."

"I wish I could convince you to eat healthier," Ms. Hall told us. "You know, thousands of years ago, people didn't have junk food. Cavemen actually had a very healthy diet."

"And look what happened to *them*," I told her. "They all died. Maybe if those cavemen ate some Twinkies, they'd still be around today."

Why do grown-ups like veggies so much? We used to have a health teacher named Ms. Leakey. She opened up a restaurant called McLeakey's that had nothing but apples. But then she was fired when she was caught sitting in a Dumpster eating junk food.

"How about tasting zucchini, dollface?" Ms. Hall said to me. "It's delicious, and it's good for you. Here, I'll cut you a slice."

Ms. Hall started cutting the zucchini into little pieces and passing them around. Only Andrea ate some.

I don't get it. Why would a sliced zucchini taste any different than an unsliced zucchini? It's still zucchini, any way you slice it.

"No thanks," I said. "I'm sticking with junk food."

"I'll convince you, dollface," she said. "I'm really good at that. But for now, I need to go run the dishwasher."

What? A dishwasher can't run. It doesn't even have legs. And even if it did, why would you want it to run? I say dishwashers should stay in one place, like refrigerators.

We were almost finished with lunch when Emily came back to the table.

"I was thinking, Emily," said Andrea. "You and I should start the Veggie Lovers Club."

"That's a great idea!" said Emily.

"You only want to start the Veggie Lovers Club so Ms. Hall will like you," I told Andrea.

"That's not true, Arlo," said Andrea. "I'm starting the Veggie Lovers Club because I love veggies."

"Oh, yeah?" I said. "Well, if you're going to start the Veggie Lovers Club, we're going to start the Veggie *Haters* Club!"

"Yeah!" said Ryan, Michael, Neil, and Alexia. Everybody was excited. Starting a new club is fun.

"I have an idea," said Alexia. "The first thing we should do in the Veggie Haters Club is to have a boycott."

"Why?" I asked. "I'm not tired."

"All the boys have to sleep on cots?" asked Ryan.

"No, dumbheads!" said Alexia. "A boy-cott is when a group of people refuse to do something. Like, we can just refuse to eat veggies for the rest of our lives."

"That's a *great* idea!" said Neil. "Let's boycott veggies!"

"Yeah!" we all shouted.

Alexia should get the Nobel Prize. That's a prize they give out to people who don't have bells.

Nice Try, Ms. Hall

After school, we had the first meeting of the Veggie Haters Club in my backyard. We took a vote, and everybody decided I should be president of the club. We made Alexia vice president.

So if I dropped dead, she would be president. If Alexia and I both dropped dead, Ryan would be president. Then if

Ryan dropped dead, Michael would be president. And if Michael dropped dead, Neil would be president. And if *all* of us dropped dead, we'd form the Dead Veggie Haters Club.

"I call the first meeting of the Veggie Haters Club to order," I announced.

"Clubs always have a mission statement," said Alexia.

"How about 'We hate veggies,'" suggested Neil.

"All in favor, say aye," I said. "All opposed, say nay."*

"Aye!" everybody shouted.

That was easy. We decided that the first

---

*That makes no sense at all. Why do we have to make horse noises?

order of business for the Veggie Haters Club would be to have a protest march in the vomitorium. I got some cardboard and markers so we could make signs.

DOWN WITH PLANT EATERS, I wrote on my sign.

NO-CARROT ZONE, wrote Alexia.

SPINACH IS FOR LOSERS, wrote Michael.

BEAT BEETS, wrote Ryan.

LETTUCE NOT EAT VEGGIES, wrote Neil.

We rolled up our signs and hid them in our backpacks. I couldn't wait until lunchtime the next day, when we would march around and show everybody our signs.

When we got to the vomitorium for the big protest march, Ms. Hall was in the hall-way with Dr. Brad, our school counselor. They were whispering back and forth.

"It looks like they're telling secrets," Alexia said.

"What are they saying?" I asked. "I can't read lips."

"They're probably making a secret plan to get us to eat veggies," said Michael.

"Well, we're not doing it!" I said. "Right, gang? Because we're the Veggie Haters Club!"

"That's right!" said Alexia. "We'll show *them*!"

We pulled out our signs and marched

around the vomitorium. It was cool. Some kids were cheering us. Some were booing.

I noticed the room looked different. All the veggies were at the front of the food line instead of at the end. They were in colorful bowls. And there were signs on the walls: **VEG OUT WITH VEGGIES! VEGGIES TASTE GREAT! V IS FOR "VEGGIES"!**

We sat at a table and took out our peanut butter and jelly sandwiches. Emily and Little Miss Perfect came over and sat with us as usual. They are so annoying. Ms. Hall rang a little bell to get everybody's attention.

"Today is Rainbow Day," she announced.

"Any student who eats at least three colors of veggies at the salad bar is eligible to win a prize: two tickets to DizzyLand!"

"WOW!" everybody shouted, which is "MOM" upside down. DizzyLand is an amusement park where they have like a million hundred rides, and at least half of them can make you throw up.

"I hope I win!" Andrea said as she and Emily rushed over to the salad bar.

I wasn't going to fall for that. I started eating my peanut butter and jelly sandwich. After a while, Ms. Hall came over to our table.

"How about trying a tomato, dollface?" she said, holding one up.

The tomato had a little sticker on it. There was a picture of Striker Smith on the sticker. He's a superhero from the future who travels through time and fights bad guys.

"Striker Smith is awesome!" said Ryan.

"And I bet Striker Smith loves tomatoes," said Ms. Hall.

Nice try!" I told her. "But we're the Veggie Haters Club. We don't eat veggies, ever! We don't care *what* you put on them."

But Ms. Hall wasn't giving up.

"Hey dollface, check this out," she said as she pulled something from her pocket. I thought it was going to be another veggie, but it wasn't. It was a bunch of baseball cards. Instead of having baseball players on them, they had pictures of veggies.

Ms. Hall handed me a card with a picture of broccoli on the front. I turned it over. On the back, it had a bunch of facts about broccoli. . . .

- Broccoli helps fight cancer.
- Thomas Jefferson planted broccoli in his backyard.
- The guy who made the James Bond movies was named Broccoli.

"Here," said Ms. Hall, "each of you can have a card. Collect them all. Swap them with your friends."

Those cards were cool. They almost made me want to try a bite of broccoli. *Almost.*

"No way!" I told Ms. Hall as I gave her back the card. "We're not falling for your little tricks to get us to eat veggies. Right, gang? The Veggie Haters Club stays strong!"

"That's right!" everybody shouted.

So nah-nah-nah boo-boo on Ms. Hall.

Ms. Hall Is in a Pickle

After lunch, we had recess. We were playing on the monkey bars when Ms. Hall came over and pulled me aside.

"Can you and I chew the fat for a minute?" she asked.

"Uh, okay," I said.

"I'm not trying to butter you up here,

dollface. But I know you are one smart cookie."

"Thank you, I guess," I said.

"You and your club have given me some food for thought," Ms. Hall told me. "I realize that veggies are not your cup of tea."

"No. I don't like them."

"Well, I'm going to spill the beans to you," said Ms. Hall.

"Huh?" I said, which is also "huh" spelled backward.

What beans? I didn't see any beans. What did beans have to do with anything? And why would she spill them on purpose?

"Veggies are my bread and butter," Ms. Hall explained. "I'm working for peanuts here. But I need to bring home the bacon."

What?

"So you should probably get some bacon and bring it home," I replied.

"What I'm trying to say," Ms. Hall told me, "is that I thought this job was going to be a piece of cake."

Huh? A job and cake are two completely different things.

"I mean," she continued, "I thought being the lunch lady at your school would be like taking candy from a baby."

"Why would you want to take candy

from a baby?" I asked. "That's not very nice."

"I thought it would be easy as pie," replied Ms. Hall. "I'd be able to have my cake and eat it too."

Why was she talking about cake so much? I thought she loved veggies.

"But it turned out that this has been a hard nut to crack," Ms. Hall continued. "Maybe I bit off more than I could chew."

I looked to see if she had some food in her mouth. But she wasn't chewing anything.

"I guess my eyes were bigger than my stomach," she said.

"How do you know how big your stomach is?" I asked. "It's inside your body."

"Anyway," Ms. Hall said, "now I'm in a pickle."

"You are?" I asked, looking around. I didn't see a pickle. How could anybody fit in a pickle anyway?

"My goose is cooked," said Ms. Hall.

"Then I guess you should take it out of the oven so it doesn't burn," I told her.

"I have egg on my face," said Ms. Hall.

She did not. I definitely would have noticed that. She must be a really sloppy eater.

"I guess now I'll have to eat crow," she said. It almost looked like she was going to cry.

"Maybe it will taste like chicken," I said, trying to make her feel better.

"I just can't cut the mustard here."

Who cuts mustard? Can't you just squirt it out of the bottle?

"I guess I laid an egg," she said.

What? People don't lay eggs. Chickens do.

"This will be a bitter pill to swallow," she told me. "But I guess life isn't a bowl of cherries."

Huh? What do cherries have to do with anything?

"If I can't get you and your friends to eat veggies," said Ms. Hall, "it will be back to the salt mines for me."

It must have been weird to go from working in a salt mine to being a lunch lady. That was some career change.

"But that's the way the cookie crumbles," she said.

She has cookies? I'd eat some of those.

"There's no use crying over spilled milk," she told me.

"You should call Miss Lazar, the custodian," I said. "She loves cleaning up messes."

"But I wanted you to know that I'm not a bad egg," she said. "And if I can get you and your friends to eat veggies, well, that will be icing on the cake. I'll be top banana around here. The big cheese. It will be the best thing since sliced bread."

"Uh . . . okay."

"So, I guess that's it in a nutshell," she said. "That's the whole enchilada."*

Huh? What's an enchilada?

---

*Wow, she sure uses a lot of food idioms!

"Well, anyway, this was a good chat," said Ms. Hall. "Thanks for listening, doll-face."

"Uh, yeah. Sure. I guess."

I had no idea what she was talking about. Ms. Hall is a goofball.

Ugh, Gross! Disgusting!

When I got to school the next day, the weirdest thing in the history of the world was going on. All the kids in my class were out on the grass talking to Ms. Hall. Even Mr. Cooper was out there. He was wearing overalls and holding some shovels and rakes.

"What's going on?" I asked. "Are we digging for gold?"

"No," Ms. Hall replied. "We're planting a
garden!"

WHAT?!

Ms. Hall told us to start digging and hoeing and raking the dirt so she could plant seeds for the garden. It was hard work.

"How much are we getting paid for this?" I asked, leaning on my shovel.

"Your pay is the joy that will come from growing your own food," said Ms. Hall.

Ugh. Growing food is disgusting. Why would anybody want to eat something that came out of the dirt?

"Aren't there laws against this?" said Alexia as she wiped her forehead with her sleeve.

We worked for a million hundred hours in the garden. I thought I was gonna die. That's when the weirdest thing in the history of the world happened. Suddenly the school bus pulled up to the curb.

Well, that's not the weird part. The school bus pulls up to the curb every day. The weird part was what happened next.

"Bingle boo!" hollered our bus driver, Mrs. Kormel. "Limpus kidoodle!"

That means "hello" and "have a seat." Mrs. Kormel is not normal. She invented her own language.

"Where are you taking us?" Alexia asked as we climbed on the bus.

"You're going on a field trip," she said.

"Yay!" everybody shouted.

Field trips are cool. One time, we went to a museum that had an exhibit called "The World of Poop."

"Where is the field trip?" I asked Mrs. Kormel.

"We're going to a farm," she replied.

WHAT?!

Farms are boring. All they have there are plants and animals.

We drove a million hundred miles. Ms. Hall told us that from now on, all the fruits and veggies we get for lunch will be coming from local farms. We got a tour of the farm, and Ms. Hall explained how they grow spinach, carrots, green beans, and other veggies. What a snoozefest.

At the end of the tour, Ms. Hall showed us how to milk a cow. It was gross. I can't believe milk comes out of a cow. I thought it came out of a supermarket. I'm never

going to drink milk again.

By that time, we were all getting hungry for lunch. And you'll never believe what was in the parking lot at the farm.

It was a food truck!

Food trucks are trucks that have food in them. So they have the perfect name. Food trucks are cool. Everybody knows food tastes way better when it comes from a truck.

Ms. Hall said we could order anything we wanted and that she would pay for it. I ran over to the window of the food truck so I'd be first in line.

"I'll have a hot dog," I said.

"We have tofu dogs," said the lady. "This is a *vegetarian* food truck."

WHAT?!

Me and the rest of the Veggie Haters Club sat down at a picnic table and pulled out the peanut butter and jelly sandwiches we brought from home.

"You know, Arlo," Andrea said as she walked by munching a stalk of celery.

"Peanut butter and jelly *is* vegetarian."

"It is not," I said.

"It is too," said Andrea. "It doesn't have meat in it, does it?"

Andrea smiled the smile she smiles to let everybody know that she knows something nobody else knows. She thinks she is *so* smart because she's a member of PAC. That's the Principal Advisory Committee—a group of nerds who get to boss around the principal.

Ms. Hall came over to our table. She had a knife in one hand and a big cucumber in the other.

"Hey," she said, "do you kids know what goes really well with peanut butter?

Cucumbers! They have lots of vitamins and minerals, and they're good for your skin and heart. You can slip a slice of cucumber into your sandwich and you won't even taste it."

"No thank you," I said. "We hate veggies."

"A cucumber is ninety-six percent water, dollface," said Ms. Hall, "so it's hardly like eating a veggie at all."

"You know, that cucumber doesn't look half bad," Ryan said.

"Try it, Ryan," said Ms. Hall, cutting off a slice of cucumber for him.

"Don't do it, Ryan!" I shouted.

"Just take one bite," said Ms. Hall, handing it to him. "It won't kill you."

"Stay strong, Ryan!" I yelled.

"It looks so *good*," Ryan said as he took the slice of cucumber.

"You're a founding member of the Veggie Haters Club!" Alexia hollered.

Ryan looked at me. I looked at Alexia. Alexia looked at Michael. Michael looked at Neil. Neil looked at Ryan. Ryan opened his mouth.

"I thought you were loyal!" shouted Michael.

Ryan put the cucumber slice in his mouth.

"Noooooooo!" all the members of the Veggie Haters Club screamed.

Ugh, gross! Disgusting! RYAN ATE CUCUMBER!

"Hey, this is good!" Ryan said. Then he took another bite. Then he asked for another slice. Ms. Hall smiled.

I knew Ryan would crack. He'll eat

anything. One time, he ate a piece of the seat cushion on the school bus. It was only a matter of time until he ate a veggie.

"You are officially kicked out of the Veggie Haters Club," I announced angrily. "Take your cucumber and leave!"

Look down.*

---

*Ha! Made you look down!

You Should Have Been There!

We were pretty mad at Ryan. I couldn't believe that one of my best friends and a founding member of the Veggie Haters Club would eat a veggie. I will never speak to him for the rest of my life.

The next morning, we were in Mr. Cooper's class. He told us to turn to page twenty-three in our math books when an announcement came over the loud-speaker.

"MR. COOPER'S CLASS, PLEASE REPORT TO THE CAFETORIUM."

Hmmm. That was weird. It wasn't lunchtime yet.

We walked a million hundred miles to the vomitorium. Ryan—that traitor—went to sit at a different table with some other plant eaters.

Ms. Hall rolled out on her roller skates. She was wearing a big chef's hat.

"Welcome to cooking class!" she said. "Today I'm going to show you how to roast veggies."

WHAT?!

"We don't care if they're roasted," I said. "We're not eating *any* veggies! Right, gang?"

"Right!" shouted Alexia, Michael, and Neil.

"You don't have to eat *anything*, dollface," said Ms. Hall. "But watch this!"

She rolled over to a big table that had onions, carrots, asparagus, and other yucky veggies on it. Then the most amazing thing in the history of the world happened. Ms. Hall picked up three knives and started juggling them!

"WOW!" we all said, which is "MOM" upside down.

Ms. Hall tossed a tomato in the air and sliced it in half as it fell. That was cool. Then she started chopping up all the other veggies. She was spinning around on her roller skates, flinging veggies, and juggling knives all at the same time. The table must have had a built-in oven, because soon the veggies were sizzling and smoking.

At the end of the show, Ms. Hall flipped a bunch of carrot slices up in the air with a spatula and caught them in her chef's hat. It was amazing! You should have been there! And we got to see it live and in person.

We all clapped our hands in circles to give Ms. Hall a round of applause.

That show was really impressive. But I wasn't going to eat carrots just because Ms. Hall can flip them into her hat.

"Who wants a carrot slice?" she asked.

"Me!" shouted the plant eaters.

Ms. Hall told them to open their mouths. Then she flipped carrot slices into their mouths from across the room. Cool!

"Those carrots actually smell pretty good," Michael said.

"Don't be tempted, Michael," Alexia told him. "Remember, you belong to the Veggie Haters Club. We don't eat veggies. *Ever.*"

"Mmmmm!" said Andrea. "Roasted carrots are yummy!"

Michael reached his hand out toward a piece of roasted carrot.

"The force," he said, "is . . . very . . . powerful."

"Don't switch over to the dark side, Michael!" I yelled.

"I can't help it, man," Michael groaned. "I want to eat one."

"Noooooooooo!" I shouted, just before Michael put a piece of carrot in his mouth.

He chewed it for a few seconds, and then he swallowed it.

"I like it!" he said. "I like carrots! I'm sorry, A.J."

Ms. Hall smiled.

"You are out of the Veggie Haters Club!" I shouted at Michael. "I will never speak to you again for the rest of my life."

Look down.*

_____

*Ha-ha! Made you look down again!

A Surprise Visitor

Michael and Ryan were now officially out of the Veggie Haters Club forever. After school, Neil, Alexia, and I held an emergency meeting in the playground. We put our hands together the way sports teams do before a big game.

"I solemnly swear," we all said, "we will

stick together through thick and thin. We will refuse to eat veggies no matter what."

On Monday morning, we were in Mr. Cooper's class.

"Turn to page twenty-three in your—"

He never got the chance to finish his sentence because an announcement came over the loudspeaker.

"ALL GRADES, PLEASE REPORT TO THE ALL-PURPOSE ROOM."

"Not again!" shouted Mr. Cooper.

We walked a million hundred miles to the all-purpose room, which should really have a different name because you can't ride dirt bikes in there. I sat with Neil and Alexia.

That's when the weirdest thing in the history of the world happened. Purple smoke started pouring onto the stage. The sound of drums pounded out of the speakers. Then the lights went out, and laser beams started shooting around in all different colors.

The drums got louder! The lights got brighter! And you'll never believe who jumped up onto the stage.

I'm not going to tell you.

Okay, okay, I'll tell you. It was Mr. Hynde, our old music teacher! He left our school after he appeared on *American Idol* and became a famous rapper.

"Gimme a beet!" Mr. Hynde shouted.

We all started making beatboxing sounds.

"No, not a *B-E-A-T*," shouted Mr. Hynde. "A *beet*! Gimme a *B-E-E-T*!"

Ms. Hall came running over and handed him a beet. Mr. Hynde ate it. Then he started break dancing and spinning on his head. Then he started rapping. . . .

"You say tomatoes. Well, so do I.

I'd rather eat tomatoes than apple pie.

All the teens like to eat their greens,

and my favorite one is lima beans.

I like dill and I always will.

You'll never fail if you eat kale.

I'll always finish my plate of spinach.

Black-eyed peas, if you please.

I'll take a glass of that wheat grass.

I got no stress when I eat watercress.

Only a bumpkin don't love pumpkin.

Cauliflower gives me the power.

Don't be a weenie. Just eat a zucchini.

I won't hustle. My sprouts are Brussels.

Just don't shriek when I take a leek.

I'm not joking, I'm artichoking."

Everybody was going *crazy*. Mr. Hynde was out of his mind! He started beating on Mr. Klutz's bald head like it was a bongo drum. The rest of our teachers made a line behind Mr. Hynde and started kicking their legs up like the Rockettes. Ms. Hall was roller-skating around and dancing. It was cool, and I saw it with my own eyes!

Well, it would be pretty hard to see something with somebody else's eyes.

"What a spectacle!" Neil said.

That made no sense at all. What did glasses have to do with anything?

We all stood up to give Mr. Hynde a standing ovation.

After that, Ms. Hall roller-skated around

the all-purpose room with a basket.

"Who wants a veggie?" she shouted, tossing little red tomatoes, rutabagas, and other veggies into the crowd.

"Me!" the plant eaters shouted. "I do!"

"Not me!" said me and Alexia.

I looked over at Neil. He wasn't saying anything.

"Uh . . . ," Neil finally said. "I . . . uh . . ."

"No!" I yelled at Neil. "Don't do it!"

"But watching Mr. Hynde rap makes me want a veggie!" Neil said.

"You're in the Veggie Haters Club!" Alexia shouted at him. "Doesn't that *mean* anything?"

"We took an oath, Neil!" I told him. "We swore we would be veggie haters for life!"

Ms. Hall came over and handed Neil a beet.

"Don't do it!" I shouted desperately.

Neil put the beet in his mouth.

"Noooooooooo!"

"Ummm," he said. "Yum!"

Ms. Hall smiled.

"You are banished from the Veggie Haters Club *forever,*" I told Neil angrily. "I will never speak to you again for the rest of my life."

Look up.*

---

*Why did you look down? I told you to look up!

Pepper Poppers and Turbo Tomatoes

Now the Veggie Haters Club was just me and Alexia. Everybody else had joined the ranks of the plant eaters. This was the worst thing to happen since TV Turnoff Week.

The next day at lunch, Alexia and I sat at our own table in the corner. We were both feeling sad. I didn't even enjoy my sloppy joe.

"Carnivores!" shouted my ex-friends at the other table.

"Herbivores!" Alexia and I shouted back.

Ms. Hall had a big smile on her face as she roller-skated around the vomitorium with a big cardboard box.

"Who wants snacks?" she hollered.

"We do!" shouted all the plant eaters.

Ms. Hall was tossing out little bags of stuff. Then she got to our table.

"How about you two?" she asked. "Would you like a snack, dollface?"

"No thank you," I said politely. "I don't eat veggies."

"Oh, these aren't veggie snacks," Ms. Hall replied. "These are *junk food* snacks."

"Junk food snacks?" asked Alexia.

Ms. Hall reached into the box she had been carrying and pulled out a bag. It looked like a bag of potato chips. It said "Kale Krunchies" on it, and there was a picture of a kangaroo.

"Hmmm, those look good," Alexia said.

"Don't even *think* about it," I told her.

"That kangaroo is cute," Alexia said, "and the chips look kind of like junk food."

"They're cool ranch flavored," said Ms. Hall. "You'll love 'em!"

"It's a trick," I told Alexia. "They just made those veggies look like junk food to get us to eat them. Don't be fooled."

Ms. Hall reached into the box.

"Let's see," she said, going through the other snacks. "I've got X-Ray Carrots, Turbo Tomatoes, Broccoli Bombs, Cool Cucumbers, Pepper Poppers, Mean Green Bean Machines, Mississippi Munchies, and Zucchini Zambonis."

"Hmmm . . . ," said Alexia.

"I'll tell you what," said Ms. Hall. "I'll give each of you a dollar if you just take one bite. One *little* bite."

"That's not fair," I told Ms. Hall. "That's a bribe!"

"Yes, it is," Ms. Hall replied. "I'm so desperate that I'll bribe you kids to eat veggies."

"Oh, yeah?" I said. "Well, we wouldn't eat a veggie if you paid us a *million* dollars. Right, Alexia?"

"You'll give me a dollar if I take *one bite*?" asked Alexia.

"One little nibble," said Ms. Hall.

"I can use the dollar to buy candy," said Alexia.

"Don't do it!" I told her.

Ms. Hall took a dollar from her pocket and dangled it in front of Alexia's face.

Alexia took the bag of Cool Ranch Kale Krunchies.

She ripped it open.

Then she put a chip in her mouth.

"Noooooooooo!"

Ms. Hall smiled.

Rebel without a Cause

Well, that was that. All my friends had abandoned me. There was only *one* person left in the Veggie Haters Club.

Me.

Who needs the rest of those plant eaters anyway? Let 'em eat their veggies, I say. Nobody's gonna tell *me* what to put in my mouth.

The next morning in Mr. Cooper's class, we pledged the allegiance and did our word of the day. Then we had math. Then we had social studies.

I was starting to get hungry for lunch.

Then we had fizz ed. After that, we had reading.

"Isn't it time for lunch yet?" I asked Mr. Cooper.

"Lunch is going to be a little later today," he told me.

Then we had science. Then we had spelling.

My stomach was starting to rumble. I looked at the clock. It was after one. We usually eat at twelve o'clock.

"Can we go to lunch now?" I asked Mr. Cooper.

"Soon," he replied.

Then we had library. Then we had computer class.

It was almost two o'clock! Soon it would be time for dismissal. I was *starving*. I didn't know how long I could hold out without

food. I was starting to feel sleepy. I thought I might pass out right there at my desk.

"Lunchtime!" Mr. Cooper announced.

"Finally!" I said, grabbing my lunch box. We pringled up and walked a million hundred miles to the vomitorium. When we got there, I staggered over to a table in the corner all by myself.

"Need . . . food," I moaned. "Going . . . to . . . die."

Ms. Hall was walking around with a bowl filled with snap peas.

"Who wants veggies?" she shouted.

"I do!" all the plant eaters were yelling.

"No thanks," I said. "I have a peanut butter and jelly sandwich."

That's when the weirdest thing in the history of the world happened. I opened my lunch box.

Well, that's not the weird part. I open my lunch box every day. The weird part was what happened when I looked *inside* my lunch box.

MY PEANUT BUTTER AND JELLY SANDWICH WAS MISSING!

Noooooooo!

This was the worst thing to happen since National Poetry Month! I wanted to run away to Antarctica and go live with the penguins.

I fell off my chair and started crawling across the floor.

"Need . . . food!" I groaned. "So . . . hungry! I'm . . . starving!"

"Mmm, these snap peas are really good, A.J.," said Ryan.

"Yeah, you should try 'em," said Michael.

"Come on, doll face," said Ms. Hall. "Give peas a chance."

Then she started singing, and soon everybody in the vomitorium began singing with her.

"All we are saying . . . is give peas a chance."

Ms. Hall got down on her hands and knees, putting her face right next to mine.

"You know you want it, dollface," she whispered, holding a snap pea a few inches from my mouth. "You want it *bad*."

I was so hungry. I didn't know what to say. I didn't know what to do. I was

faced with the hardest decision of my life.
Everybody in the vomitorium was looking
at me.*

   "Okay, okay!" I shouted. "You win!"

---

*Isn't this exciting? I bet you're on pins and needles. Well,
you should get off them. That must hurt.

I opened my mouth.

Ms. Hall put the snap pea in my mouth.

I chewed it.

I swallowed it.

It was totally silent in the vomitorium. Everybody was on the edge of their seats.

Well, not really. They were just sitting in the middle of them, like always. But there was electricity in the air.

Well, not exactly. If there was electricity in the air, we would all have been electrocuted. But it was *really* exciting!

"So?" said Ms. Hall. "What do you think, dollface?"

"Not bad," I replied. "Can I have another one?"

Well, that's pretty much what happened. I guess I'm a plant eater now.

Maybe I'll speak to my old friends in the Veggie Haters Club again. Maybe Ms. Hall will stop calling me dollface. Maybe she'll stop running dishwashers and bring home the bacon instead of taking candy from babies and eating crows. Maybe Ms. LaGrange is locked up in the freezer. Maybe we'll find out what the mystery meat is. Maybe beasts will come to the city. Maybe we'll have to eat Vinkies and food made out of toes. Maybe they'll start selling peppers with toys inside them and portable meat spray in a can. Maybe Ms.

Hall will stop juggling knives and tossing carrot slices into her hat. Maybe cavemen will start eating Twinkies. Maybe Ryan and I will dig a hole to China so we can get some shrimp lo mein. Maybe all the boys will have to sleep on cots. Maybe I'll win tickets to DizzyLand. Maybe they'll let us ride dirt bikes in the all-purpose room. Maybe Ms. Hall will get out of her pickle, clean the egg off her face, and learn how to cut the mustard so she doesn't have to work in a salt mine anymore.

But it won't be easy!

 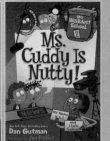

My Weirdest S

Mr. Will Needs to Chill!

Dan Gutman

Pictures by
Jim Paillot

HARPER

An Imprint of HarperCollinsPublishers

To Emily Borowicz

My Weirdest School #11: Mr. Will Needs to Chill!

Text copyright © 2018 by Dan Gutman

Illustrations copyright © 2018 by Jim Paillot

All rights reserved. Printed in the United States of America.

No part of this book may be used or reproduced in any manner whatsoever without written permission except in the case of brief quotations embodied in critical articles and reviews. For information address HarperCollins Children's Books, a division of HarperCollins Publishers, 195 Broadway, New York, NY 10007.

www.harpercollinschildrens.com

ISBN 978-0-06-242942-1 (pbk. bdg.)—ISBN 978-0-06-242943-8 (library bdg.)

Typography by Laura Mock

19 20 21 22 BRR 10 9

❖

First Edition

Contents

The Ding-Dong Man

My name is A.J. and I hate ice cream.

Well, I don't hate *all* ice cream. I like *normal* ice cream, like vanilla, chocolate, strawberry, and mint chip. But my friend Billy, who lives around the corner, told me he likes *weird* ice cream flavors like bacon, garlic, and octopus. What's up with *that*? Why would anybody want to eat octopus-flavored ice cream? What dumbhead dreamed up that idea?

You probably think this book has nothing to do with ice cream, but you're wrong. It has *everything* to do with ice cream.

You see, it was Friday, and we just pledged the allegiance in Mr. Cooper's class like we do every morning. That's when an announcement came over the loudspeaker. It was our principal, Mr. Klutz.

"Good morning, Ella Mentry students," he announced. "It's a sunny day today. Lunch will be sloppy joe sandwiches. There are no birthdays today. The big news is that Mrs. Jafee and I are leaving this morning to go to Principal Camp."

Oh, yeah. Every year, Mr. Klutz and our vice principal, Mrs. Jafee, go hang out in the woods for a few days with a bunch of other principals. Nobody knows why.

"We're going to learn all kinds of new and creative teaching methods to help you kids learn better," said Mr. Klutz.

Oh, so *that's* why they're going to Principal Camp. I wondered who would be our principal while Mr. Klutz and Mrs. Jafee were gone.

"While we're gone," Mr. Klutz continued, "the acting principal will be Dr. Marshall Carbles, the president of the Board of Education."

Oh no! Not Dr. Carbles! He's the meanest man in the history of the world.*

"Have a nice weekend!" announced Mr. Klutz. "I'll see you when I get back from Principal Camp."

---

*If you don't believe me, read *Dr. Carbles Is Losing His Marbles!*

It was hard to focus on reading and writing and math. I kept thinking about mean Dr. Carbles.

It was also hard to focus on reading and writing and math because it's *reading and writing and math*. It would be a lot easier to focus on video games, skateboarding, and football. Too bad we don't study *those* things in school.

Finally it was time for recess, the best part of the day. Me and the gang ran out to the playground to play on the monkey bars. That's when we heard a tinkling sound.

You know the sound I'm talking about?* It's the greatest sound in the world. It's the

---

*No, not that sound! That's *another* tinkling sound.

5

Ding-Dong truck coming down the street!
Everybody stopped what they were doing.

"It's Mr. Will, the Ding-Dong man!"
shouted Michael, who never ties his shoes.

"Mr. Will, the Ding-Dong man!" shouted
Ryan, who will eat anything, even stuff
that isn't food.

"Mr. Will, the Ding-Dong man!" shouted
Alexia, this girl who rides a skateboard all
the time.

In case you were wondering, everybody was shouting that it was Mr. Will, the Ding-Dong man.

Mr. Will is the greatest man in the world, because he drives the Ding-Dong truck. It's a truck filled with ice cream! What could be greater than that? Anybody who has a truck full of ice cream must be great.

Mr. Will probably gets to eat all the ice cream he wants, every day. Wow! That's my dream job. When I grow up, I'm going to drive an ice cream truck and be a Ding-Dong man.

We ran over to the fence and pressed our faces against it.

"I *love* ice cream," said Andrea Young, this annoying girl with curly brown hair.

"Me too," said Emily, her copycat cry-baby friend.

"*Everybody* loves ice cream," said Neil, who we call the nude kid even though he wears clothes.

It was true. Who doesn't love ice cream?

"I can smell the ice cream from here," I said.

"You can't *smell* ice cream, Arlo," said

Andrea, who calls me by my first name because she knows I don't like it. "Ice cream doesn't have a smell."

"It does too."

"Does not."

We went back and forth like that for a while.

"Your *face* has a smell," I told Andrea.

"Oh, snap!" said Ryan.

Mr. Will was playing my favorite song, the Ding-Dong ice cream jingle. It goes like this. . . .

Do do do do do do do do do do
do do do do do do do do do do

Or something like that.

Mr. Will plays the Ding-Dong jingle over and over and over, all day long.

"When I was little," Michael told us, "my parents called the Ding-Dong truck 'the music truck.' They said it just drives around all day playing music. They didn't tell me it had ice cream in it."

"*My* parents said that when the music was playing, it meant the Ding-Dong man ran out of ice cream," said Alexia.

"Parents are weird," I said. "They'll do anything to prevent us from eating ice cream."

Mr. Will parked the Ding-Dong truck on the street across from the playground. So near and yet so far away. He leaned out of the truck and waved to us. He was wearing his white Ding-Dong uniform. I really wanted to go over and get some ice cream, but we're not allowed to leave the school grounds during recess. It's not fair!

That's when the most amazing thing in the history of the world happened.

I'm not going to tell you what it was.

Okay, okay, I'll tell you. But you have to read the next chapter. So nah-nah-nah boo-boo on you.

The Great Escape

Suddenly a bunch of our teachers came running out to the playground. In front of all of them was Dr. Carbles.

"What is that racket?" he shouted.

Racket? I didn't see a racket anywhere. Our school doesn't even have tennis courts.

"It's Mr. Will, the Ding-Dong man," somebody said.

"Turn off that horrible noise!" hollered Dr. Carbles. He and the teachers were holding their hands over their ears.

Oh, yeah. The Ding-Dong jingle drives grown-ups crazy. Nobody knows why.

"I can't take it!" shouted Dr. Carbles. "Make that awful music stop!"

It seemed like a good time to start chanting.

"WE WANT ICE CREAM!" I hollered. "WE WANT ICE CREAM!"

I thought the rest of the kids would join in and start chanting with me. But nobody did. I hate when that happens.

"Get that truck out of here!" Dr. Carbles shouted at Mr. Will. "Go peddle your sugary junk food someplace else!"*

Mr. Will stepped out of the Ding-Dong truck and walked slowly toward the fence. Oh, this was going to be good.

"What did you say?" asked Mr. Will.

"Beat it, Ding-Dong man!" shouted Dr. Carbles. "I'll have you arrested!"

"This is a free country," Mr. Will shouted right back. "I can go anywhere I want."

"Turn off that terrible music right *now*!" shouted Dr. Carbles.

"No!" Mr. Will shouted back.

—————————————————

*I've heard of pedaling a bike, but it would be weird to pedal ice cream.

The two of them were yelling at each other through the fence. It was awesome. Watching grown-ups argue is fun. And we got to see it live and in person.

"Don't cross me, Ding-Dong man!" shouted Dr. Carbles. "I will make you

regret the day you were born! Nobody messes with me. I'm warning you."

Then he turned around and marched back to school with the other teachers. Mr. Will went back to the Ding-Dong truck. The excitement was over.

We were going to go play on the monkey bars, but we couldn't stop staring at the Ding-Dong truck and thinking about what was inside it.

"I haven't had ice cream in a million hundred years," I said.

"You had ice cream *yesterday*, A.J.," said Michael. "I was over at your house, remember? Your mom made us banana splits."

"Well, it *feels* like that was a million hundred years ago," I said.

"I need ice cream like other people need air," said Ryan.

"I can almost taste it," said Alexia.

"If I don't have ice cream soon, I'm gonna die," said Neil.

"It's not fair," I said. "The ice cream is just sitting right there in the truck, and we can't have it."

If only there was some way to sneak out of the playground. I looked at the bottom of the fence. That's when I got the greatest idea in the history of the world.

"Look," I said. "We can tunnel our way out!"

Everybody looked at the bottom of the fence. It was a few inches off the ground.

"You're right!" said Neil. "Let's dig a

tunnel! A.J., you're a genius!"

I should get the Nobel Prize for that idea. That's a prize they give out to people who don't have bells.

"I don't know," said Andrea. "Digging a tunnel sounds dangerous, Arlo."

"Danger is my middle name," I replied.*

"I'm scared," said Emily, who's scared of everything.

"What if you get caught?" asked Andrea. "You could get in big trouble, Arlo."

"Trouble is my other middle name," I said. "Come on, guys, start digging."

Everybody got down on their hands

---

*It really isn't. But I heard somebody say that in a movie once, and it sounded cool.

18

and knees and started digging out the dirt under the fence.

"Hurry up," said Ryan. "Dr. Carbles could come back out here any second."

After a million hundred minutes, we dug out enough dirt so I could fit under the fence.

"Okay, wish me luck," I said as I started to slide under.

"Wait a minute," Michael said. "Do you have any money?"

Oh, yeah. Ice cream costs money.

Everybody emptied their pockets. Neil had four pennies. Michael had two quarters. Alexia had a quarter and some dimes. Ryan had some Life Savers. They gave it all to me.

"I don't feel good about this, Arlo," Andrea said.

"A man's gotta do what a man's gotta do," I told her.

"It was nice knowing you, A.J.," said Alexia. She put her hand on my shoulder. I thought she might cry.

"If I don't make it back alive," I told her, "you can have my skateboard, Alexia."

Ryan and Michael pulled up the bottom of the fence a little so I could fit under it.

"I'm going in, guys," I said.

"If you don't make it back, Arlo," said Andrea, "I will always remember you."

"Oooooh!" Ryan said. "Andrea said

20

she'll always remember A.J. They must be in *love*!"

"When are you gonna get married?" asked Michael.

If those guys weren't my best friends, I would hate them.

I slid under the fence and climbed out the other side. I was free!

Ice Cream Is Ice Cream

I ran over to the Ding-Dong truck and pulled the coins out of my pocket.

"I need ice cream!" I shouted to Mr. Will. "Fast!"

"Well, you came to the right place, A.J.," he replied. "What can I get for you?"

"I'm in a hurry," I said. "I'll just have an ice cream cone."

"Great!" said Mr. Will. "Chocolate or vanilla?"

"Chocolate."

"Soft serve or hard ice cream?" asked Mr. Will.

"Soft."

"Wafer, waffle, or sugar cone?" asked Mr. Will.

"Wafer," I told him. "Can we move this along?"

"Dipped or undipped?" asked Mr. Will.

"Undipped."

"Sprinkles?" asked Mr. Will.

"Sure. Whatever."

"Chocolate or rainbow sprinkles?" asked Mr. Will.

"Rainbow. Either way. I don't care."

"There's just one problem, A.J.," said Mr. Will.

"What's the problem?" I asked.

"I don't have any ice cream cones today."

WHAT?!

"Why didn't you tell me that before?"

"You didn't ask," said Mr. Will.

On the other side of the fence, the gang was shouting for me to hurry up. I looked at the little pictures of ice cream on the side of the Ding-Dong truck.

"Okay," I told Mr. Will. "I'll have a crushed cherry sundae."

"Sorry. I'm all out of those," he replied.

"How about a lemon berry slushie

float?" I asked Mr. Will.

"Just sold the last one."

"Popsicle? Fudgsicle? Creamsicle? Dreamsicle?" I asked Mr. Will.

"Out of stock."

"Milk shake? Ice cream sandwich? Banana boat?"

"Nope."

"Turbo Rocket? Choco Taco? Dip-n-roll?" I asked Mr. Will.

"Not today. Sorry."

I wasn't getting anywhere. Time was running out. Recess would be over soon.

"Well, what kind of ice cream *do* you have?" I asked Mr. Will.

"Let me see . . . ," he said, looking into

the freezer. "How about an octopus Push-Up pop?"

"Octopus?" I said. "Ugh!"

"It's not octopus *flavored*," said Mr. Will. "It just *looks* like an octopus."

"Okay, okay," I said. "I'll take anything. Ice cream is ice cream."

"That will be seventy-nine cents," said Mr. Will.

I'm good at math. I pulled out three quarters and four pennies and gave him the coins. He handed me the octopus Push-Up pop. I started running back to the fence.

But I couldn't resist. I had to take a bite of the Push-Up pop first. I stopped for a second and ripped off the wrapper. The Push-Up pop was a beautiful thing, with red and blue swirls. I was about to take my first bite.

That's when the weirdest thing in the history of the world happened. Suddenly I heard a loud siren and whistles behind me.

"Hands up!" a voice shouted through a bullhorn. "We've got you surrounded!"

I put my hands in the air.

"Drop the Push-Up pop and nobody gets hurt!" the voice shouted.

I turned around. It was Dr. Carbles!

I've seen enough movies in my life to know that when somebody tells you to drop what you have in your hand, you

should always say, "Who's gonna make me?"

"Who's gonna make me?" I asked.

"I am!" shouted Dr. Carbles.

I've seen enough movies in my life to know that when somebody says they're going to make you, you should always say, "You and what army?"

"You and what army?" I asked.

"Me and *this* army," shouted Dr. Carbles.

At that moment, a bunch of big goons in military uniforms came around the corner. They looked mean, and they had some angry, barking dogs with them.

I've seen enough movies in my life to know that when an army actually shows up, you should always shout, "You'll never take me alive!" And then you should make a run for it.

"You'll never take me alive!" I shouted. And then I made a run for it.

I was heading for the hole under the fence.

"Get him, boys!" shouted Dr. Carbles. "Release the dogs!"

I didn't know what to do. I didn't know what to say. I had to think fast.

"Run for your life, A.J.!" shouted Neil.

Everybody was yelling and screaming and shrieking and hooting and hollering and freaking out as I ran back to the fence.

Dr. Carbles's goons and their dogs chased me. They grabbed me just before I got back to the hole we dug.

"Up against the fence, A.J.!" shouted Dr. Carbles. "Step away from the Push-Up pop."

"Okay! Okay! I give up!"

Marshall Law

4

You probably think Dr. Carbles locked me in a torture chamber and pulled my eyelashes out one at a time and set my toenails on fire. Well, he didn't do any of those things. He just made me write this a hundred times in my notebook. . . .

*I will not sneak under the fence and
go get ice cream from the Ding-Dong
truck. I will not sneak under the fence
and go get ice cream from the Ding-
Dong truck. . . .*

Bummer in the summer! It took me all
weekend to finish. My hand hurt! It was
the worst weekend of my life. I wanted to
go to Antarctica and live with the penguins.

When I got to school on Monday morning, something was different. There was
barbed wire across the top of the playground fence. At each corner of the school,
there was a guard tower. The guard towers

had security cameras and searchlights on them. Mean-looking goons in uniforms were patrolling the playground with attack dogs.

"This is *bad*," said Ryan when I saw him on the front steps.

"It looks like Dr. Carbles is turning our school into a prison," said Neil.

"How do you think he got those guard towers over the weekend?" asked Michael.

"He must have gone to Rent-A-Guard Tower," I guessed. "You can rent anything."

"I hope Mr. Klutz and Mrs. Jafee come back from Principal Camp soon," said Alexia.

We went inside the school and walked a million hundred miles to Mr. Cooper's class. He didn't look happy and excited like he usually does. He just sat at his desk staring off into space. That's when the morning announcements came over the loudspeaker. It was the voice of Dr. Carbles.

"It will be cloudy and depressing today," he announced. "Lunch will be dried mush. There are no birthdays today, or ever again. Birthdays are for losers."

WHAT?!

"Boooooooooooooo!" everybody started shouting.

"There will be *no* sneaking over to the Ding-Dong truck during recess," continued Dr. Carbles. "From now on, recess is canceled. Recess is for losers."

WHAT?!

"Boooooooo!"

"Maybe we can go to the Ding-Dong truck after school lets out this afternoon," Michael whispered hopefully.

"And you can forget about going to the Ding-Dong truck after school lets out," Dr. Carbles announced. "I got a restraining order against Mr. Will. He isn't allowed to come within five hundred feet of the school anymore. So *nobody* gets ice cream. Not on *my* watch."

What did watches have to do with anything? Why would anybody put ice cream on a watch? That would be weird.

"I wonder when we'll be allowed to get

ice cream again," whispered Emily.

"You can forget about getting ice cream for the rest of your *life*," announced Dr. Carbles.

WHAT?!

"Boooooooo!"

"Wow, it's almost as if Dr. Carbles can hear us talking," whispered Andrea.

"I heard that!" said Dr. Carbles. "Mr. Cooper's students had better stop whispering to each other, or they'll all be in big trouble!"

"He put a bug in our classroom!" whispered Andrea.

"Gross!" I shouted, looking inside my desk. "I hate bugs."

"Not *those* kinds of bugs, dumbhead," said Andrea. "Dr. Carbles planted a microphone somewhere in here. He's listening to every word we say."

"That's right," said Dr. Carbles. "So you'd better watch your p's and q's."

Huh? Why should we watch *those* letters? It didn't make any sense.

"I'm afraid," said Emily, who's afraid of everything.

But I was afraid too. We all were.

Finally the morning announcements were finished. I looked over at Mr. Cooper to see what he was going to teach us. But he just sat there with his head on the desk.

"What are we going to work on this

morning, Mr. Cooper?" asked Andrea. "Social studies?"

"No."

"Reading?" asked Alexia.

"Nah."

"Do you want us to turn to page twenty-three in our math books?" asked Ryan.

"Whatever," groaned Mr. Cooper. "I don't care."

That was weird. Mr. Cooper *loves* teaching us stuff.

After a few minutes he told us it was time for fizz ed with Miss Small. Yay! I love fizz ed. We walked a million hundred miles to the gym. When we got there, Miss Small didn't look very happy either. She was sitting on the floor under the basketball hoop.

"Are we going to play basketball this morning, Miss Small?" I asked.

"No."

"Are we going to have relay races?" asked Alexia.

"No. Just go out in the playground and do whatever you want," Miss Small muttered. "I'm not in the mood."

Wow. None of the teachers wanted to teach! With Dr. Carbles in charge, they just looked sad.

So we did what we were told. We went out to the playground. And you'll never believe in a million hundred years what happened next.

There was that sound in the distance.

A jingly-jangly sound.

It was . . . the Ding-Dong truck!

"He's back!" I shouted. "Mr. Will is back!"

"Hooray!" everybody shouted as the Ding-Dong truck pulled up and Mr. Will stepped out of it.

That's when the weirdest thing in the

history of the world happened.

A tank came rolling down the street.

Not a fish tank. It would be weird if a fish tank came rolling down the street. No, it was one of those army tanks, with a cannon in front. I saw it with my own eyes!

Well, it would be pretty hard to see something with somebody *else's* eyes.

The tank stopped close to the Ding-Dong truck. The hatch on the top opened up. And guess whose head popped out of it? Yes, it was Dr. Carbles's!

"You are breaking the law, Ding-Dong man!" he shouted through his bullhorn. "Get out of here, and turn off that horrible music!"

"No way!" Mr. Will shouted back. "Did you ever hear of the First Amendment?

We have freedom of speech in this country, you know!"

"Your freedom of speech ends at my ears!" shouted Dr. Carbles.

"Your students want ice cream!" shouted Mr. Will.

"I don't care what my students want!" Dr. Carbles shouted back. "If you don't get out of here right this minute, I will *make* you leave."

It looked like there was going to be a big fight. Like maybe Mr. Will was going to shoot soft serve ice cream out of a hose on the Ding-Dong truck. That would be cool.

"I don't like violence," said Andrea. "It's

inappropriate for children."

"What do you have against violins?" I asked her.

"Not violins, Arlo! Violence!"

I knew that. I was just yanking Andrea's chain.

But there was no battle. Mr. Will didn't spray Dr. Carbles with ice cream. He just walked back to the Ding-Dong truck and slowly drove away.

"Don't come here again!" Dr. Carbles shouted as he shook his fist in the air at Mr. Will. "I will crush your pathetic ice cream rebellion."

There was nothing we could do but watch through the fence. Dr. Carbles turned around and looked at us.

"Go back to class, you little punks!" he barked.

He's mean! Having Dr. Carbles as our principal was worse than TV Turnoff Week. It was worse than National Poetry Month. It was worse than TV Turnoff Week and National Poetry Month *put together.*

As Mr. Will drove off, we could hear the Ding-Dong jingle fading away in the distance. For the first time ever, it sounded sad and lonely.*

---

*This is the sad part of the book. Get some tissues, will you? You're slobbering all over yourself.

Dried Mush and Cold Gruel

It was really quiet when we got to the vomitorium for lunch that day. Everybody was afraid of what Dr. Carbles might do next.

Me and the gang waited in line until we reached Ms. LaGrange, our lunch lady. Ms. LaGrange is strange. One time, she wrote a secret message in the mashed potatoes. That was weird.

"What's for lunch, Ms. LaGrange?" asked Michael.

"Today I'm serving a bowl of dried mush with a piece of stale bread," she replied sadly.

The mush looked gross.

"Mush is a food?" asked Alexia.

"It is *now*," Ms. LaGrange replied. "I'm under direct orders from Dr. Carbles. And tomorrow we will have cold gruel."

"Gruel? What's that?" asked Neil.

"You don't want to know," Ms. LaGrange replied.

"Can we get dessert?" I asked.

"Dessert?" said Ms. LaGrange with a

snort. "Are you kidding?"

"No dessert?" I asked.

At that moment, a voice came out of a little speaker next to the cash register.

"Dessert is for losers!" said the voice. "Eat your dried mush and stop complaining! You kids are lucky to get any food at all."

It was Dr. Carbles! There was a little video camera next to the cash register.

"I've got my eye on you, A.J.," Dr. Carbles said. "Don't try any funny stuff or you'll be in big trouble."

We found an empty table and sat down. I looked at my bowl of dried mush.

"I'm not eating this," I said.

"Me neither," said everybody else.

Except Ryan, of course. Ryan will eat anything, even stuff that isn't food.

"I'll try it," he said.

Ryan dipped his spoon into the dried mush.

Then he brought the spoon up to his lips.

I was already grossed out.

Then Ryan opened his mouth.

I thought I was gonna die.

Then Ryan put the spoon in his mouth.

Isn't this exciting?*

---

*Here's a tip for all you writers out there. If you want a story to sound exciting, all you need to do is put each sentence on a line by itself. That's the first rule of being an exciting writer!

Then Ryan swallowed the dried mush. Ugh, gross!

I looked at Ryan. Michael looked at Ryan. Andrea looked at Ryan. Neil looked at Ryan. *Everybody* was looking at Ryan.

"Not bad," Ryan finally said. "It tastes like pudding."

Pudding?! We all dipped our spoons into the dried mush. Actually it wasn't bad once you put some sugar on it.

But even so, everybody was in a bad mood during lunch. Recess had been canceled. After we finished eating, we were told to go out to the playground, where Dr. Carbles was waiting for us.

"Are we going to play a game?" asked

Andrea hopefully.

"No!" barked Dr. Carbles. "Games are for losers. Today you're going to learn how to march."

WHAT?!

"Pringle up!" Dr. Carbles shouted through his bullhorn. "Forward, march! Left! Right! Left! Right!"

It was horrible. Marching is no fun at all. While we were marching back and forth, I looked over to see if the Ding-Dong truck was parked outside the school. It wasn't. Mr. Will was nowhere to be seen.

"Left! Right! Left! Right!" barked Dr. Carbles.

"Where do you think Mr. Will went?"

Michael whispered as we marched.

"Maybe he went to Dirk School," whispered Ryan.

Ugh. Dirk School. That's a school on the other side of town for genius kids. We call it "Dork School."

"Left! Right! Left! Right!"

"Maybe Dr. Carbles kidnapped Mr. Will and tied him up in a dungeon," I whispered. "That stuff happens all the time, you know."

"Stop trying to scare Emily," said Andrea.

"I'm scared," said Emily.

"Left! Right! Left! Right!" barked Dr. Carbles. "Marching makes you *strong*. Playing silly games makes you *weak*."

Dr. Carbles had us marching back and forth across the playground for a million hundred hours. It was horrible.

"I'm not sure I remember what ice cream tastes like anymore," Ryan whispered.

"I think it's cold and wet," whispered Michael.

"I'll never know what an octopus

Push-Up pop tastes like," I said.

"Someday we'll look back on our childhood," whispered Alexia. "We'll tell our grandchildren what ice cream tasted like."

"Those were the good old days," I whispered to Alexia.

"What, you mean yesterday?" whispered Neil.

"Left! Right! Left! Right!"

"Even if we can't eat ice cream anymore," whispered Andrea, "at least we can have frozen yogurt."

"Frozen yogurt isn't ice cream!" I whispered. "It's not the same!"

"You're right, Arlo," Andrea admitted. "Life wouldn't be worth living without ice cream."

That's when Emily started to cry. Then we *all* started crying.

Everybody was whimpering and sniffling and snorting. It was the saddest day in the history of the world.*

---

*Hey, when do the jokes start again? Isn't this book supposed to be funny? You should get your money back! That is, unless you got it from the library. Then it was free anyway.

Hooray for Mr. Klutz!

The next day when we got to school, I saw the most amazing thing. The guard towers were gone! The barbed wire was gone! So were the security cameras and the barking dogs! And most importantly, Dr. Carbles was gone! Standing at the top of the front steps and giving everyone hugs was our principal, Mr. Klutz.

He has no hair at all. I mean *none*. His head is like a bowling ball with a face on it.

"He's back!" everybody was shouting. "Mr. Klutz is back!"

Mr. Klutz is a nice man. He's not mean like Dr. Carbles.

"I missed you kids!" Mr. Klutz shouted when we all came over to hug him.

"We missed you too!" said Emily.

"Dr. Carbles is mean," said Ryan.

"Marshall can be a little . . . uh, strict," Mr. Klutz replied.

"A little?" said Michael. "He drives a *tank* to school."

"Did you have a good time at Principal Camp, Mr. Klutz?" asked Andrea.

"Oh yes," he replied. "Mrs. Jafee and I met lots of experts in the field of education, and we learned all kinds of new ways of teaching. I think it's going to help you kids learn things."

Ugh. Learning things is a drag. But at least it will be better than having mean Dr. Carbles around.

"So we don't have to march in the playground anymore?" asked Neil.

"Nope," said Mr. Klutz.

"We don't have to eat dried mush and cold gruel for lunch?" asked Alexia.

"Never again."

"Can we have recess today?" asked Ryan.

"Sure!"

"Can we go out for *ice cream* during recess?" I asked hopefully.

"Why not?" said Mr. Klutz. "In fact, you can go out for ice cream right *now*."

"HUH?" we all said, which is also "HUH" backward.

This was too good to be true! I figured

Mr. Klutz must be pulling a prank on us. We're *never* allowed to eat ice cream first thing in the morning. That's the first rule of being a kid.

"Really?" I asked. "We can have ice cream first thing in the morning?"

"Absolutely!" said Mr. Klutz. "One of the experts at Principal Camp told me that kids learn better when they eat ice cream for breakfast. He said the cold wakes up your brain.*

Hmmm, that makes sense.

"Hooray for Mr. Klutz!" everybody started chanting. "Hooray for Mr. Klutz!"

"Go ahead!" said Mr. Klutz. "I think I

---

*That is a total lie.

hear the Ding-Dong truck coming down the street right *now.*"

He was right! The Ding-Dong truck pulled up across from the school. It was playing the Ding-Dong jingle, as always.

"Ah, I love that song," said Mr. Klutz.

"Mr. Will is back!" somebody shouted.

"Hooray for Mr. Will!" everybody started chanting. "Hooray for Mr. Will!"

"Let's go get ice cream!" Alexia shouted.

"Yeah!"

We were all about to run over to the Ding-Dong truck, but then we stopped.

"Wait," Michael said. "I don't have any money."

"Neither do I," said Emily.

"I just have my lunch money," said Andrea.

"You don't need to use your own money," said Mr. Klutz.

He reached into his pocket and pulled out his wallet. Then he gave each of us a dollar.

What?! Free ice cream? First thing in the morning? This couldn't be happening! It was going to be the greatest day of my life.

We all ran over to the Ding-Dong truck. That's when the most amazing thing in the history of the world happened. The Ding-Dong truck was back, but Mr. Will wasn't inside it! It was some *other* Ding-Dong guy, with blond hair. He was wearing a white Ding-Dong uniform just like Mr. Will.

"Where's Mr. Will?" we all asked him.

"I don't know," the Ding-Dong guy said. "I guess he took the day off. I'm Mr. Bill."

Hmmm, that was weird. Well, I didn't care *what* the guy's name was. As long as he had ice cream.

"Do you have octopus Push-Up pops?" I asked Mr. Bill.

Ever since Dr. Carbles took away my octopus Push-Up pop, I had been thinking about octopus Push-Up pops.

"Sure!" said Mr. Bill as he reached into the freezer and pulled one out. "That will be seventy-nine cents, please."

I handed Mr. Bill the dollar Mr. Klutz gave me. Mr. Bill looked at the dollar bill. He had a puzzled expression on his face.

"I don't know how much change to give you," he said.

What?! That was weird. Mr. Will always gave us our change right away. It didn't even seem like he had to think about it.

"There are a hundred pennies in a dollar," I explained to Mr. Bill. "All you need to do is take seventy-nine from a hundred."

Mr. Bill looked at my dollar bill again. Then he looked at me. He still looked all confused.

"I don't get it," he said. "Can you show me how to do that?"

What?! A Ding-Dong man who can't make change for a dollar? Mr. Bill must be a real dumbhead.

"Uh, I guess so," I said.

He handed me a pad and pencil.

"Look," I told him as I wrote on the pad. "It's simple subtraction. The zero becomes a ten. Ten minus nine equals one. The other zero becomes a nine, and nine minus seven equals two. So you owe me twenty-one cents."

"Ah yes," Mr. Bill said as he handed me two dimes and a penny. "I see it now. Thanks for explaining that to me."

"No problemo," I told him.

I was about to unwrap my octopus Push-Up pop when I stopped.

"Hey," I said, "that sounded a lot like a math lesson just there. Are you a math teacher?"

"No, don't be silly," said Mr. Bill. "I'm just a Ding-Dong man."

Mr. Bill is weird.

Mr. Mill

Mr. Bill's octopus Push-Up pop was yummy. I could hardly taste any octopus at all. Ryan got a coconut Popsicle dip. Michael got a rocket pop. Alexia got a double-dipped butterscotch swirl cone. It was the greatest day of our lives.

When we got inside the school, all the

kids and teachers were smiling again. The day seemed to fly by. Mr. Klutz was right. Eating ice cream first thing in the morning *does* help you learn. At lunchtime in the vomitorium, Ms. LaGrange made yummy chicken nuggets and Tater Tots for us. Everybody was happy.

I must admit, without mean Dr. Carbles around, school was kinda fun. But don't tell the gang I said that. They would never let me hear the end of it.

The next morning, I could hardly wait to get to school. Mr. Klutz was waiting for us on the front steps.

"Can we buy ice cream again today?" Neil asked.

"Of course!" replied Mr. Klutz as he handed each of us a dollar bill. "I can hear the Ding-Dong truck coming down the street right now."

We all ran over to the Ding-Dong truck as soon as it pulled up to the curb. I was expecting to see Mr. Bill, the new Ding-Dong driver guy. But that's when the weirdest thing in the history of the world happened.

Mr. Bill wasn't in the truck! It was some *other* guy. He had red hair.

"Where's Mr. Bill?" we all asked him.

"Mr. Bill is on vacation," said the red-haired guy. "I'm Mr. Mill."

WHAT? How could Mr. Bill be on

vacation already? He just started work yesterday! Oh, well. As long as we get ice cream every morning, I don't care *who* the Ding-Dong guy is.

"I'll have a chocolate Magic Shell Bomb Pop," I told Mr. Mill.

"Sure, coming right up," he replied. "Hey, did you know we've had ice cream as far back as the second century BC?"

"Really?" I asked. "Wouldn't it be rotten by now?"

"No, I mean ice cream was invented a long time ago," Mr. Mill told me. "Alexander the Great liked to eat snow and ice flavored with honey."

"That's nice," I said. "I'll have a chocolate Magic Shell Bomb Pop."

But Mr. Mill didn't give me a chocolate Magic Shell Bomb Pop like I asked. He just kept talking.

"During the Roman Empire," he said, "Emperor Nero sent runners up to the mountains to get snow. Then he had it flavored with fruit."

"That's interesting," I said. "Can I have a chocolate Magic Shell Bomb Pop now, please?"

"Did you know," said Mr. Mill, "that Marco Polo went to the Far East and came back to Italy with a recipe for something that was very much like ice cream?"

"I didn't know that," I said. "Would you *please* give me a chocolate Magic Shell Bomb Pop?"

"By the time the United States became a country, ice cream was really popular," said Mr. Mill. "In fact, George Washington spent two hundred dollars on ice cream during the summer of 1790."

What a snoozefest! Could Mr. Mill possibly be any more boring? All I wanted was to eat some ice cream.

"You don't really *have* any chocolate Magic Shell Bomb Pops, do you?" I asked Mr. Mill.

"Sure I do!" he replied as he reached into the freezer and handed me a chocolate Magic Shell Bomb Pop. "Here you go."

I was about to unwrap my chocolate Magic Shell Bomb Pop when I stopped.

"Hey," I said, "that was sort of a history lesson you just gave me. Are you a history teacher?"

"No, don't be silly," said Mr. Mill. "I'm just a Ding-Dong man."

Mr. Mill is weird.

Mr. Hill

The chocolate Magic Shell Bomb Pop was awesome. I couldn't wait to get to school the next morning so I could get more ice cream from Mr. Mill. We all ran over to the truck as soon as we heard the Ding-Dong jingle.

But Mr. Mill wasn't there. It was some *other* Ding-Dong guy!

"Where's Mr. Mill?" I asked him.

"Mr. Mill is sick today," the new Ding-Dong guy told me. "I'm Mr. Hill. What would you like?"

"Can I have a Ding-Dong double-dipped Dixie Doodle?" I asked.

"Sure, coming right up," said Mr. Hill. "By the way, do you know what ice cream is made out of?"

"No," I told him. "I just like to eat it."

"Ice cream is made out of cream or milk, sugar, and sometimes eggs and flavoring," he told me. "And each molecule of sugar contains twelve carbon atoms, twenty-two hydrogen atoms, and eleven oxygen atoms."

Mr. Hill took out a pad and started drawing a weird picture. . . .

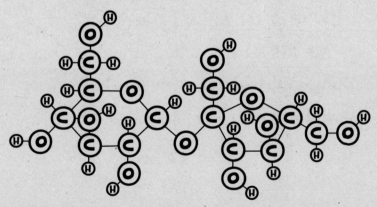

"Nice picture," I said. "Can I have my Ding-Dong double-dipped Dixie Doodle now?"

"After all the ingredients are combined, they get pasteurized," said Mr. Hill. "Do you know what pasteurized means?"

"They leave the ice cream out in a pasture for a while?" I guessed.

"No," said Mr. Hill. "That's when a liquid is heated to a very high temperature to kill off the germs, and blah blah blah blah it is cooled blah blah blah blah Louis Pasteur blah blah blah blah French scientist who invented it blah blah blah blah . . ."

He went on like that for a million hundred minutes. What a snoozefest.

"How about that Ding-Dong double-dipped Dixie Doodle?" I finally asked.

"Pasteur is famous for his discoveries blah blah blah blah helped prevent diseases blah blah blah blah germs blah blah blah . . . ," said Mr. Hill.

is. If they gave classes in toenail clipping, she would take that class so she could get better at it.

"I just don't get it," Andrea said. "I don't understand why Mr. Klutz is giving away money so we can buy ice cream. Grown-ups don't just hand out dollar bills to kids. It's not normal."

"I was wondering that myself," said Ryan. "And why is there a different guy driving the Ding-Dong truck every day?"

"Yeah, and why are all the Ding-Dong guys so weird?" asked Michael.

"Maybe they went crazy listening to the Ding-Dong jingle all day," guessed Neil. "It *does* have that effect on grown-ups."

I was going to just walk away, but suddenly Mr. Hill stopped blabbing about germs. He reached into the freezer and pulled out a Ding-Dong double-dipped Dixie Doodle for me. I took off the wrapper and had a bite. It was yummy.

"All that stuff you told me about ice cream sounded a lot like science class," I told Mr. Hill. "You're not really a science teacher, are you?"

"No, don't be silly," said Mr. Hill. "I'm just a Ding-Dong man."

Mr. Hill is weird.

The Big Surprise Ending

We got free ice cream every day! Choco-late marshmallow. Vanilla fudge ripple. Cookies and cream. You name it. It was the greatest week of my life.

You would think that everybody would have been happy. But when we were eat-ing lunch in the vomitorium on Friday,

Andrea had on her worried face.

"What's the matter?" I asked her. they cancel your clog-dancing class school today?"

Clog dancing is a dance that plur do. Andrea takes classes in *everything* school so she can show off how goo

That's it. I couldn't take it anymore. I stood up.

"What is wrong with you people?" I shouted at them. "I can't believe you're complaining. We're getting free ice cream! Every day! First thing in the *morning*! Just enjoy it!"

"I *do* enjoy it, Arlo," said Andrea. "But I'm suspicious. I think these Ding-Dong guys have some kind of a racket going on."

Huh? What did tennis have to do with anything?

"You guys are nuts," I told them. "As long as I get free ice cream every day, I'm happy."

We all went back to eating our lunch.

Nobody said anything for a while.

"But let me ask you *this*, Arlo," Andrea finally said. "What do you think happened to Mr. Will, the first Ding-Dong man? He hasn't been here all week."

Hmmm. Good question. What *did* happen to Mr. Will?

"Yeah," said Neil. "It's like he vanished off the face of the earth."*

"Maybe Mr. Will moved away," guessed Alexia. "Or maybe he got a new Ding-Dong route."

"Maybe he got fired," guessed Neil.

"Maybe he got *kidnapped*," Ryan guessed.

---

*The earth has a face? That's a new one on me.

"Yeah," I said. "Maybe all those Ding-Dong guys are *fake* Ding-Dong guys who wanted jobs with the Ding-Dong company. So they kidnapped Mr. Will, locked him up in a Ding-Dong truck, and pushed the truck over a cliff! That stuff happens all the time, you know."

"Stop trying to scare Emily," said Andrea.

"I'm scared," said Emily.

"Maybe Mr. Will is . . ."

I waited until everybody was looking at me before I finished the sentence.

". . . dead!"

"We've got to *do* something!" Emily shouted. And then she went running out of the room.

Sheesh, get a grip! That girl will fall for *anything*.

But for once in her life, Emily was right. We *did* have to do something. We had to find out what was going on.

After lunch, instead of playing outside during recess, we decided to go to Mr. Klutz's office. If anybody knew what was going on, it would be Mr. Klutz.

We walked down the hall to his office. When we got there, Mr. Klutz was sitting at his desk. He was eating an ice cream sandwich.

"Hey guys!" he said when he saw us. "Have you been enjoying your Ding-Dong ice cream?"

"Yes," Andrea said. "But we're worried about something."

"What is it?" asked Mr. Klutz. "Did the Ding-Dong truck run out of octopus Push-Up pops again?"

"No," said Andrea. "We want to know why there's a different Ding-Dong guy every day. And why are you giving away money to buy ice cream? What's *really* going on?"

Mr. Klutz didn't say anything for a while. It was like he was trying to decide how to respond.

"Okay, I admit it," Mr. Klutz finally said. "Mr. Bill and Mr. Hill and Mr. Mill are not *real* Ding-Dong guys."

"I *knew* it!" Andrea shouted.

"When I was at Principal Camp last week," Mr. Klutz told us, "I found out that kids can learn a lot when they're not in a classroom. You can learn *everywhere*. So I hired teachers to work in the Ding-Dong truck and pretend to be Ding-Dong guys. I thought it would help you learn math, history, science, and other subjects."

"It did help us!" I told him. "I learned lots of new stuff. Did you know that during the Roman Empire, Marco Polo came home and brought ice cream for George Washington's birthday party?"

"I'm not sure that's true, A.J.," said Mr. Klutz.

"Wait a minute," said Andrea. "Bringing in fake Ding-Dong guys is sort of like lying to us, isn't it?"

"Yes," Mr. Klutz admitted quietly. "I suppose you're right."

"Lying isn't nice," Andrea told him. "We're not supposed to tell lies."

"You're right, Andrea," said Mr. Klutz. "But I was trying to help you kids learn. And you did. You got to eat lots of ice cream too. So everybody comes out a winner, right?"

"Well, there's *one* person who didn't come out a winner," said Andrea. "Mr. Will."

"Yeah," Michael said. "Whatever happened to Mr. Will, the *real* Ding-Dong guy?"

"Hmmm," said Mr. Klutz as he stroked his chin.

Men always stroke their chin when they're thinking, even if they don't have a beard. Nobody knows why.

"That's a good question," he said. "I . . . honestly don't know what happened to Mr. Will."

That's when the weirdest thing in the history of the world happened. We heard a sound.

Well, that's not the weird part. We hear sounds all the time. The weird part was that the sound was coming from above, and outside. It was a muffled voice. And the voice was saying, "Help! Help!"

Mr. Klutz went to the window.

"It's coming from the roof!" he shouted. "Follow me!"

We all ran out of his office and climbed up a secret principal staircase that only principals are allowed to climb on.

"*Shhh!*" whispered Mr. Klutz when he got to the door that opened up onto the roof. "Don't make a racket!"

Huh?

"Why would anybody want to make a racket at a time like this?" I asked. "Are there tennis courts up on the roof? Why is everybody always talking about tennis rackets?"

"*Shhhh!* Quiet, Arlo!" said Andrea.

Mr. Klutz opened the door to the roof with his secret principal key. We stepped out onto the roof.

We were slinking around up there like secret agents. It was cool. Nobody said anything. You could hear a pin drop.

Well, that is, if anybody had pins with them. Who brings pins to school? That would be weird.

But anyway, there was electricity in the air.

Well, not really. If there was electricity in the air, we would have all been electrocuted. And that would hurt!

But it was really exciting. You should have *been* there!

Suddenly we heard that muffled voice again.

"Help!"

We ran over to where the sound was coming from.

And you'll never believe in a million hundred years what we found up on the roof.

Mr. Will!

"WOW!" everybody said, which is *MOM* upside down.

Mr. Will was tied to a chair. His white Ding-Dong uniform was dirty, and his hair was all messed up. He had ice cream dripping down his face, and there were Popsicle sticks on the floor around him.

"Thank goodness you rescued me!" he said.

"What happened, Mr. Will?" Andrea asked as we loosened the ropes that were tied around him.

"It was horrible!" Mr. Will said. "Dr. Carbles was mad at me for parking my truck outside the school every day and for playing the Ding-Dong jingle over and over again. So he and his goons brought me up here and left me here."

"And you've been here all week?" asked Mr. Klutz. "What did you eat?"

"Ice cream!" said Mr. Will. "I had nothing to eat but ice cream for a week."

Wait. What?

We all looked at Mr. Will.

"You had nothing to eat all week except for ice cream?" I asked.

"Yes!" said Mr. Will.

"And that's a bad thing?" asked Ryan.

"Yeah, what's wrong with that?" asked Michael.

"I'd give *anything* to eat ice cream all week," said Alexia.

"That sounds like a perfect week to me," said Andrea.

"I wish I was in *your* shoes," said Ryan.*

Only a grown-up would complain about having to eat ice cream all week.

---

*What did shoes have to do with anything? And why did Ryan want to put on Mr. Will's shoes? They would be too big. Ryan is weird.

Grown-ups are weird.

"I could have *died* up here!" Mr. Will shouted as we helped him to his feet.

Sheesh. What a whiner! If you ask me, Mr. Will needs to chill.

Well, that's pretty much what happened. Maybe Mr. Will will go back to his job driving the Ding-Dong truck. Maybe Dr. Carbles will get thrown in jail for kidnapping him. Maybe they'll start making octopus-flavored ice cream. Maybe we'll start watching our p's and q's instead of the other letters. Maybe a fish tank will come rolling down the street. Maybe Mr. Will is going to shoot soft ice cream out of a hose on the Ding-Dong truck and spray Dr. Carbles's tank with it. Maybe Ryan will start eating dried mush for lunch every day. Maybe it's true that ice cream wakes up your brain. Maybe people will stop talking about tennis rackets. Maybe Ella Mentry School will become a normal school someday.

But it won't be easy!